The Superhero Project

by Rachel Ruiz

illustrated by Steve May

PICTURE WINDOW BOOKS
a capstone imprint

Superhero Harry is published by Picture Window Books
A Capstone Imprint
1710 Roe Crest Drive
North Mankato, Minnesota 56003
www.mycapstone.com

Library of Congress Cataloging-in-Publication Data is available on
the Library of Congress website.

ISBN: 978-1-4795-9858-8 (library hardcover)
ISBN: 978-1-4795-9862-5 (paperback)

Designer: Hilary Wacholz

Printed and bound in the USA

032018 000311

TABLE OF CONTENTS

CHAPTER 1
BIRTHDAY BOY 7

CHAPTER 2
THE FIRST DAY 14

CHAPTER 3
THE ANNOYING DAY 21

CHAPTER 4
THE ASSIGNMENT 28

CHAPTER 5
THE RESULTS 35

ALL ABOUT
Superhero
HARRY

NAME: Harrison Albert Cruz

FAVORITE COLOR: red

FAVORITE FOOD: spaghetti

FAVORITE SCHOOL SUBJECT: science

HOBBIES: playing video games, inventing, and reading

IDOLS: Albert Einstein and Superman

BEST FRIEND, NEIGHBOR, AND SIDEKICK: Macy

LATEST INVENTION: Superhero Rocket Blaster Boots

CHAPTER 1

BIRTHDAY BOY

Today is super special. It is Harry's first day of school. It is also his birthday!

"Harry!" his mom calls. "Time to get up!"

But Harry has been up for an hour. He's working on X-ray vision goggles. They are his latest invention.

"Just a minute!" Harry yells.
Harry likes superheroes. He
also likes inventing things. So
Harry invents things to make
him more like a superhero.

The problem is, Harry's inventions usually don't work. The other problem is that Harry is clumsy. These are two big problems if you are trying to be a superhero.

Once Harry invented a supersonic flying machine. He used it to fly off his bed. And he fell flat on his face.

Another time Harry made superhero suction shoes. He used them to climb to the top shelf of the hall closet to look at hidden presents.

But the suction on the shoes
didn't stick. Down went Harry.

But these failures don't stop
Harry. He needs super inventions to
be a superhero. Superheroes don't
give up, and neither does Harry.

"Amazing Macy to Superhero Harry. Come in, Superhero Harry. Over."

"Copy that, Amazing Macy. Superhero Harry here. Over," Harry replies.

Macy lives in the apartment building next door. In addition to being Harry's neighbor, she's his superhero sidekick, classmate, and best friend.

"Superhero Harry, you have an incoming. I repeat, you have an incoming. Over," Macy says into her walkie-talkie.

Harry's happy to see that
Macy is using the pulley system
he invented last week.

When the bucket reaches Harry's window, he pulls out a card. It is covered with glitter glue and superhero stickers.

"Thanks, Macy!" Harry shouts.

"Use your walkie-talkie!" she yells back.

"Thanks, Macy! Over!" Harry says into his walkie-talkie.

"See you at the bus stop. It's going to be a super day! Over and out!" Macy says.

"It's the first day of school AND my birthday," Harry says. "How could today be anything but super?"

CHAPTER 2

THE FIRST DAY

At school Ms. Lane crowns Harry student of the day. The entire class sings to him. He even gets to pass out birthday treats at the end of the day. While everyone is eating, Ms. Lane makes an announcement.

"I have your first assignment," she says.

"Already?" Macy says.

"Yes, already. How are you a superhero in your everyday life?" Ms. Lane asks. "That is your assignment. Make a presentation to show the class on Friday."

That doesn't give me much time, Harry thinks.

"Everyone will vote on the best presentation. The winner will get a special prize," Ms. Lane says.

The final bell rings. Harry can't wait to get home. He'll get to open gifts and eat cake. Then he can start his superhero project!

***

"A real live inventor set!" Harry says as he opens a gift. "It says I can invent my own robot! Thanks Mom and Dad!"

"It's my turn!" Aunt Gwen says.

Harry opens her gift and starts screaming with excitement.

Aunt Gwen's gift is the most beautiful thing Harry has ever seen. It's a shiny red superhero cape. It has a gold lightning bolt on the back.

"Harry, this cape will give you superpowers," Aunt Gwen says. "You just have to believe in yourself."

"For real live life?" Harry asks.

"For real live life," Aunt Gwen says, smiling.

"I'm going to use the cape to help me win the superhero assignment contest at school," Harry says.

"What are you going to do?" his dad asks.

"Oh nothing much," Harry says. "Just invent my greatest superhero invention ever!"

CHAPTER 3

THE ANNOYING DAY

The next morning Harry is really tired. He stayed up too late working on his project.

"Harry! Wake up! You're going to be late for school!" Mom yells.

Oh, no! Harry overslept! He jumps out of bed and puts on his favorite shirt. As he puts his arm through the sleeve, it rips. Harry quickly finds another shirt.

"Harry! The bus is here!" his mom calls.

Harry zooms to the kitchen. As he runs out the door, his mom hands him a muffin.

Harry tries to stuff his superhero cape into his backpack as he rushes toward the bus. But the zipper breaks. His cape tumbles out. It lands in a mud puddle.

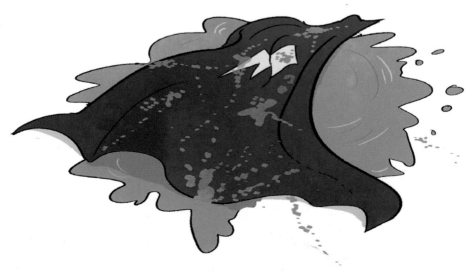

"Oh, no!" Harry says. He picks up the cape and tries to clean it off. It doesn't work. And now he has mud all over his shirt too.

Once on the bus Macy waves Harry over. Harry dumps his stuff on the seat.

"What happened to your shirt?" Macy asks.

"Don't ask," Harry says as he sits down, right on his muffin.

Things do not get better at school. Harry trips in the hall. He drops his lunch tray. He forgets his math homework. Harry is so glad when the final bell rings.

* * *

At dinner Harry tells his parents about his tough day.

"Sounds like quite a day," his mom says.

"It really was. But it's time to put that behind me. I need to focus on my superhero invention. It's going to be the best! I know I'm going to win," Harry says.

"I'm glad you're taking your assignment so seriously," his mom says. "But I think you may be missing the point."

"The point?" Harry asks.

"Your teacher asked how you're a superhero in your *everyday* life," Harry's dad says. "I think she's looking for something regular people can do."

"It doesn't have to be an invention," his mom adds.

"Sorry, Mom and Dad," Harry says. "Miss Lane asked about superheroes, and superheroes use superpowers. It's just that simple."

CHAPTER 4

THE ASSIGNMENT

"Who would like to give the first presentation?" Ms. Lane asks.

Macy and Melanie jump right up. Melanie takes her shoes off.

"Macy and I are on the same gymnastics team," Melanie says. "For weeks I've been trying to do a back handspring. I just couldn't get it. Macy helped me practice every day until — "

"She learned how to do it!"

Macy yells.

Melanie does her back

handspring. Macy stays close

by in case she needs help.

"Wonderful, girls!" says Ms. Lane. "You're both superheroes. Macy helped a friend with her goal. And Melanie worked hard and didn't give up."

Violet reads a story about helping her grandmother clean her house.

Ethan sings a song about cleaning up the park with his scout group.

They all did the assignment wrong, Harry thinks. *You can't be a superhero if you don't use superpowers!*

Finally it is Harry's turn.

He carries a box to the front
of the room. He pulls out a pair
of shiny silver puffy boots. They
each have lightning bolts and
a battery pack.

"These are my superhero rocket blaster boots. They will blast me to the moon. Or at least really, really high," Harry says.

"Cool!"

"Let's see Harry!"

"Turn them on!"

"Blast to the moon!"

Harry beams. He puts on his cape. He slips into the boots and turns on the battery packs. He stands tall. And he waits.

And waits some more.

Nothing happens.

"Let me try that again," Harry says. He turns the battery packs off and on.

But still, nothing happens. He looks at his classmates. Everyone is staring at him.

"I don't understand," Harry says. "I really thought they would work."

Harry knows he will never win the contest now.

THE RESULTS

Ms. Lane counts all the votes. The winner for the best superhero assignment presentation is Elle.

Elle showed she's a superhero by organizing a sock drive. She got people to donate socks for people in need. She collected more than 100 pairs!

Ms. Lane calls Harry up to
her desk.

"Do you understand why you
didn't win?" she asks.

"Because my rocket blaster boots didn't work," Harry says. "But they are really cool."

"Harry, your boots are very cool," Ms. Lane says. "But they didn't show me how you *really* are a superhero."

"But Ms. Lane," Harry says, "they are my *superhero* rocket blaster boots. They have the word *superhero* in the actual name!"

"Harry, being a superhero isn't just about inventions. It is about helping others," Ms. Lane says.

Harry thinks about all of the presentations. Each one was about someone helping someone else. Maybe his parents were right after all.

"So you don't have to have superpowers to be a superhero?" he asks.

"Nope. You can be a hero in a lot of ordinary ways," Ms. Lane says. "Do you understand?"

"That makes sense," Harry says. "But I'm still going to make inventions and try to fly and all that kind of stuff."

"And that's what makes you so super, Harry," his teacher says. "You never give up."

"Of course not!" Harry says. "See you tomorrow, Ms. Lane. Superhero Harry, over and out!"

GLOSSARY

assignment — a job or duty that is given to someone

clumsy — moving or doing things in an awkward way and tending to drop or break things

invention — a useful new device

presentation — an activity in which someone shows, describes, or explains something to a group of people

pulley — a wheel or set of wheels that is used with a rope to lift or lower heavy objects

sidekick — a person who helps and spends a lot of time with someone

suction — the act or process of removing the air to cause something to stick to a surface

supersonic — faster than the speed of sound

TALK ABOUT IT

1. Why does Harry like inventing things? Talk about a time when you invented or created something.

2. Harry's teacher assigns homework on the first day of school. Do you think that's fair? Why or why not?

3. Why doesn't Harry win the Superhero Assignment contest at school?

WRITE ABOUT IT

1. Write a paragraph describing what it means to be a superhero.

2. Make up your own superhero name and power. Why did you pick your name and power?

3. Write a paragraph describing how you are a superhero in everyday life.

ABOUT THE
AUTHOR

Rachel Ruiz is the author of several children's books. She was inspired to write her first book picture book, When Penny met POTUS, after working for Barack Obama on his re-election campaign in 2012.

When Rachel isn't writing books, she writes and produces TV shows and documentaries. She lives in her hometown of Chicago with her husband and their daughter.

ABOUT THE ILLUSTRATOR

Steve May is a professional illustrator and animation director. He says he spent his childhood drawing lots of things and discovering interesting ways of injuring himself.

Steve's work has become a regular feature in the world of children's books. He still draws lots but injures himself less regularly now. He lives in glamorous north London, and his mom says he's a genius.

BE A SUPERHERO AND READ THEM ALL!

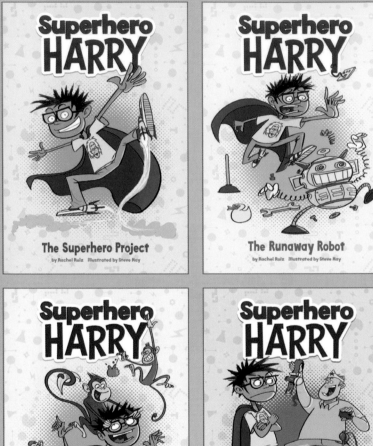

ONLY FROM capstone